Archie and
he Babysitter

First published in 2012
by Wayland

Wayland
338 Euston Road
London NW1 3BH

Wayland Australia
Level 17/207 Kent Street
Sydney, NSW 2000

Series Editor: Louise John
Series design: Paul Cherrill
Design: Lisa Peacock
Consultant: Shirley Bickler

A CIP catalogue record for this book is available from the British Library.

ISBN 9780750268691

Printed in China

Wayland is a division of Hachette Children's Books,
an Hachette UK Company

www.hachette.co.uk

Archie and the Babysitter

Written by Anne Rooney
Illustrated by Ann Johns

WAYLAND

Mum and Dad were going out for the afternoon.
Emma came to babysit.

"You can't go out now!"
Archie shouted.

"Don't be silly," Dad said.
"Emma will look after you."

"Shall we go to the park?"
Emma asked, but Archie
shook his head.

"Shall we play a game?"
Emma asked.
"No!" said Archie.

"I'm going to watch TV,"
Archie said, and he flopped
on the sofa.

Archie watched a police show about a kidnapping. "I wish it was exciting here," he said.

Archie went to find his sister, Lucy. “Let’s play hide and seek,” he said. “You hide first.”

Archie pushed her into a cupboard and Lucy screamed!

"Be quiet," Archie said. "Just hide."

Then he called Emma.
"I can't find Lucy anywhere.
She's been kidnapped! Call
the police!" he shouted.

Emma ran up and down the street. She looked all around the house.

She looked under the beds, behind the doors and in the...

...cupboards.

"Here she is!" called Emma.
"Good hiding, Lucy."
She gave Lucy a hug.

Archie flopped on the sofa
and watched TV.

He watched a show about an obstacle race.

Archie went outside. He piled up logs and filled the sandpit with water and crocodiles.

Archie used lots of things from the shed. He put lions and tigers in the bushes.

Archie pulled Lucy outside.
"Come and try my obstacle race," he said.

Archie and Lucy jumped over logs.

They ran along planks.

They swung from ropes.

Lucy fell in the water and
started to cry.

Archie ran to find Emma.
"Come quick! Lucy has fallen in the crocodile river!"

Emma wrapped Lucy in a towel and gave her a hug. “Please be good.” Emma said to Archie.

“Being good is boring!” said Archie. He flopped on the sofa to watch TV again.

He watched a hospital show. Someone was very ill. Doctors crowded around the bed.

Archie got the face paints.
He made himself green.
Then he added some spots.

"I don't feel well, Emma,"
he said.

“Oh no,” said Emma. “You look awful, Archie.” She got a blanket and some medicine.

"It's not that bad!" Archie shouted when he saw the pink medicine.

"Open wide," said Emma.

"Hello!" called Mum. "Look, we got you pizza for being good. Who was good?"

"Lucy was good," Emma said. "Archie is ill. Pizza will make him sick."

“I’m fine now!” shouted Archie and he wiped off the spots.

“Oh, Archie!” said Dad. “You are awful!”

START READING is a series of highly enjoyable books for beginner readers. The books have been carefully graded to match the Book Bands widely used in schools. This enables readers to be sure they choose books that match their own reading ability.

Look out for the Band colour on the book in our Start Reading logo.

The Bands are:

START READING books can be read independently or shared with an adult. They promote the enjoyment of reading through satisfying stories supported by fun illustrations.

Anne Rooney has written lots of books for children including the All About Henry stories for this series. Have a look! She lives in a state of chaos with her two daughters, a tortoise called Tor2 and a blue lobster called Marcel.

Ann Johns likes to draw life – busy, lovely life. Birds flying, dogs jumping, people dancing... So always have a pencil handy, because you never know what exciting thing is waiting around the corner for you to draw!